MAISIE GOES TO SCI

Author and Illustrator: Aileen Paterson

This story is dedicated to my grandsons, Koto and Tariye.
With thanks to Mrs Irene Milner and all the children who requested a
school story.

© Aileen Paterson

Published in 1988 by
The Amaising Publishing House Ltd.
Musselburgh
EH21 7UJ
Scotland

031-665 8237

Reprinted 1993
Printed & Bound by Scotprint Ltd, Musselburgh

ISBN 1 871512 01 8

Other Maisie Titles in the Series:

Maisie and the Posties

Maisie's Festival Adventure

Maisie loves Paris

Maisie and the Space Invader

What Maisie did Next

Maisie in the Rainforest

Maisie goes to Hospital

Maisie and the Puffer

One Monday morning, very early, Maisie woke up with a start. Her new alarm clock was ringing, making the most awful noise! She tried pulling the covers over her head, but it was no use. She reached out, switched the alarm bell off and peered at the dial.

Big hand at twelve, little hand at seven. Seven o'clock! For a moment or two, being a wee bit drowsy, she couldn't remember why she had to be up so early. Then it came to her in a flash.

Today was her first day at school!

There had been great excitement in Granny's house for weeks.
What a lot of things kittens need for school!
Granny had taken her to a big store in Princes Street to buy her uniform.

A navy-blue blazer, and a badge to sew on the pocket. White blouses. A tie.

Grey wool for Granny to knit into cardigans.
A Lunchbox with Supercat on it.

A red and yellow school-bag which would glow in the dark on winter mornings to warn traffic that Maisie was on her way to school.

When they wrote to tell Daddy the news he sent Maisie a pretty pencil box, filled with pencils with her name stamped on them in gold, a ruler, and a pencil-sharpener.

He sent her a nice letter too.

Dear Maisie,
 I'm so pleased to hear that you are starting school. What a big grown-up kitten you will be. I'm very proud of you. Remember to send me a photograph of yourself in your school uniform to pin up in my tent. Maybe you'll learn to swim. I've been swimming in a lake in the mountains in Tibet. What a treat it was, which is more than I can say about the tea here. Tell Granny they don't put sugar in, or milk, just lumps of very old butter made from yak's milk! It's **AWFUL**. Be good, and write soon,
 Lots and lots of love
 from Daddy.

P.S. This is what a yak looks like.

A YAK.

Now the great day had arrived.

Maisie jumped out of bed, washed, and dressed herself in her school clothes. Granny tied the tie for her. Then she went into Granny's bedroom to admire herself in the long mirror. It was true, she thought, she was very grown-up.

After breakfast, Granny popped a packet of prawn crisps in the school bag, a play-piece she called it. Mrs McKitty, up and about sweeping the stair and polishing her doorknob, came in and gave her a final inspection.

"I must say, Maisie, you do look very smart—a credit to your Granny," she said.

Praise from Mrs McKitty was praise indeed. Maisie's heart swelled with pride.

Paw in paw up the brae went Granny and Maisie, past the shops, past Holy Corner and the three big churches, towards the school crossing. There stood the Lollipop Cat. His name was Mr Rafferty, and he was an old friend of Granny's.

"Hello, Maisie," he cried. "So you're one of my new customers, eh? It's a busy road this, so take care. Wait for the wee green cat to shine on the traffic light!"

As they crossed, he sang a song to remind her about ROAD SAFETY.

> *Oh, Maisie it's the Rule*
> *When on your way to school,*
> *To always cross with Mr Rafferty,*
> *The cars all have to stop*
> *When they see my Lollipop,*
> *So you will be as safe as safe can be.*

Granny laughed as they waved good-bye to Mr Rafferty, and said he was a "real cough-drop" and a great favourite with all the kittens.

They went into the school and there, waiting for them with some of her new class, was Miss Purrvis, Maisie's teacher.

Maisie thought she looked very pretty.

Granny had a few words with Miss Purrvis, then she kissed Maisie good-bye and said she would be back to collect her at lunch-time.

Miss Purrvis led her little band of kittens into their classroom, and their schoolday began.

Granny walked down the road feeling a wee bit wobbly. It was a big day for her, too.

Mrs McKitty invited her in for a coffee when she got home.

"Dearie me," sighed Granny. "The house is going to be very quiet without Maisie. I do hope she settles down at school. She's such a lively little soul."

Mrs McKitty offered Granny one of her delicious home-made Petticoat Tails as she stirred her coffee.

In her opinion Maisie was more than just lively—explosive was more like it—but this wasn't the time to say so. Instead, she told Granny about her niece, Lydia MacSporran of Lady Road, and how quickly she had settled into school last year.

"Brains run in our family as you know, Isabella, and Lydia is no exception. Her work books are full of ticks, and so many gold stars they fairly dazzle you!"

Granny went away home to do her housework, not very comforted.

At lunchtime she collected Maisie and took her home. Maisie was very hungry. She tucked into a big bowl of broth and a plate of mince and tatties, then sat back.

"That feels better," she said. "School is hard work, you know."

And she told Granny all about her first day at school.

"I've got a peg to hang my blazer on and a drawer to keep all my things in.

None of my friends are in my class!

Flora and Hector go to a different school—The Kittens' Academy. Archie's in my school, and so is Effie, but Archie's in Miss Catkin's class, and Effie's in the Nursery.

I've got a nice new friend called Anna though. We sit at the same table."

"We drew pictures, then we made plasticine sausages and snakes. I got some in my fur, but Miss Purrvis got it out. We had milk and a story, and at Playtime I learned skipping with a big rope. I'm quite tired out!"

Granny, whose morning had been filled with cooking, cleaning, and shopping, was highly tickled—and very pleased that Maisie had enjoyed herself.

Maisie soon recovered from this hard-working morning. She went out to collect Granny's paper, "The Evening Mews". When she came back she looked excited.

"Take your paws and cover your eyes; Count to three and you'll get a surprise!", she told Granny.

Granny counted to three. When she opened her eyes, there on her lap was her paper, and on the front page was a picture of Maisie's class!

Maisie had kept her secret well.

A reporter had visited the school and taken their photograph! Granny was very thrilled. She sent Maisie out for two more "Evening Mewses"—one for Mrs McKitty, and one for Daddy, of course.

Evening Mews

NO. 523910　Price 20 pence　MONDAY 23rd AUGUST

PUPILS ENJOY THEIR FIRST DAY AT SCHOOL.

BY STAFF REPORTER— SCOOP GIBSON

HAPPY FACES ALL AROUND AT MORNINGFIELD PRIMARY SCHOOL AS THEY BEGIN LIFE AS SCHOOL KITTENS. CLASS 1B SEEN HERE WITH THEIR TEACHER MISS PURRVIS.

STOCKBRIDGE CAT HAS TWELVE KITTENS!

MOTHER AND LITTLE ONES DOING WELL.

STOP PRESS: THIRTEENTH KITTEN ARRIVES IS THIS A RECORD FOR EDINBURGH CAT?

HOORAY FOR HOLYROOD!

TOURISTS FLOCK TO HISTORIC PALACE, HOME OF MARY, QUEEN OF CATS.

* * * * * * * * * * * * * *

CAT BURGLAR CHASED BY LEITH POLICE

TERRIBLE TAM LANDED IN DOCK TODAY. HE WAS FOUND AFTER LONG CHASE, BY TWO LEITH BOBBIES. IN HIS PAWS WERE TWO PIZZAS, A LOBSTER & FOUR PIES.

COD WAR!

HERRINGS WERE IN A PICKLE IN FIRTH OF FORTH WHEN CHASED BY A GIANT COD.

Festival Fun ★

It take two to Tattoo! Two seats for the price of one. See the Siamese Sand Dance and Catford Pipers tonight

* * * * * * *

Fishguard Chamber Orchestra in Concert at Usher Hall. SCHUBERT'S TROUT QUINTET Conductor Leo CATGUT.

SIAMESE QUEEN WEDS BARNTON GROOM.

MORNINGSIDE KITTENS LOSE THEIR MITTENS 24 PAIRS FOUND IN DOMINION CINEMA.

MANAGER WELCOMES THE OWNERS TO LOST & FOUND DEPARTMENT

LATEST

HEARTS V. HIBS CUP FINAL!

BOOK FESTIVAL

KITTENS ARE RUSHING TO CHARLOTTE SQ. SEE PAGE 27.

T.V Tonight

CBI
5 BLUE POINT
5 NEWS
9 CATS CRADLE
10 BOOK CHOICE "MAISIE"
11 FILMS FOR PUSSIES.

S.C.T.V
5 CARTOON
6 SCOT NEWS
7 SERIAL. "TAKE THE FERRY ROAD"
8 NAME THAT YEOWL
9.
10 NEWS.

CH4½
5 TOP KAT
5 VET TIME
7 NEWS
8 CAT-SOAP
9 FISH PRICES
10 GOODNITE

CBC2
FILM: "CAT DANCING (FRED AND GINGER) 9. FLOYD ON FLOUNDERS. 10. NEWSNITE 11. BYE BYE.

Maisie went to school every day after that. Sometimes she walked up with Granny, sometimes with the big kitten who lived upstairs. He was at the High School.

But she wasn't settling down quite as well as Granny had hoped. She liked school. She liked Miss Purrvis and Anna. She liked sums, reading, "choosing!" and playing in the Wendy House. She liked eating her packed lunch with her friends. But somehow, she kept getting into mischief. She didn't really mean to be naughty . . . it just sort of happened.

One day her class went into the gym to do some exercises. Miss Purrvis played the piano while the kittens touched their toes and bent and stretched. Maisie got a bit tired of all this hard work. She noticed some thick ropes tied on the wall and decided to have some fun.

She untied one, climbed up it, and began swinging backwards and forwards above the heads of the other kittens.

They all started to giggle and laugh, especially when Maisie made Tarzan noises!

Miss Purrvis looked out from behind the piano. She was not very pleased.

She marched them all back to the classroom and gave Maisie a telling-off.

Maisie was good for quite a long time after that, then her high spirits got her into trouble again.

There was a school rule painted on the wall outside.

NO FOOTBALL ALLOWED
IN THE PLAYGROUND.

Maisie broke the rule!

She took her ball outside at Playtime to show off to Anna her skills as a footballer. At first she just dribbled the ball around the other kittens' paws, but then she got carried away.

"Watch this," she cried, "I can score goals with my head!"

She bounced the ball, then headed it high in the air—but it flew sideways and crashed through one of the school windows.

Maisie was horrified. The playground went quiet. Kittens rushed from every corner to see the big hole in the window.

Suddenly a big cat in a brown coat appeared, carrying the ball in his paws. All eyes turned to Maisie. There was no need for him to ask which kitten had done the dreadful deed.

"Get into your lines, the whole jing-bang lot of you," he cried. Then he turned to Maisie.

"Not you, young lady. Follow me".

He took her into his office and showed her the glass scattered on the floor. She helped him sweep it up, and said she was very sorry.

She told him about her Granny, and about all the reports they heard from Mrs McKitty about Lydia MacSporran's good behaviour.

He wondered what Mrs McKitty would say when she heard about Maisie's latest disaster.

"Are you the Headmaster?", she asked him timidly.

He smiled down at her.

"No, no, Maisie," he said. "I'm Mr Whiskers, the janitor—a very important person. Now run along to your teacher, and try to keep out of bother. Mind now!"

Miss Purrvis sent a note home to Granny, and a bill for the new window. Maisie paid for it out of her savings. Mrs McKitty talked about nothing else for a whole week. Poor Granny! Poor Maisie!

She began to work very hard at school and Miss Purrvis was very pleased with her. Gold stars appeared in her work book! Mrs Brown, the Art teacher, pinned one of her pictures up on the wall! It looked as if Maisie was settling down at last . . .

Then, one morning, Maisie was given messages to do. She had to take a note to Mr Whiskers to order the morning milk for her class.

She went along to his office, but he wasn't there. Instead of leaving the note on his table like the other kittens had done, Maisie decided to go and look for him.

The door to the school swimming pool was open and she heard Mr Whiskers inside, whistling, so she ran in. Just as she came in one door, Mr Whiskers went out of the other one to fetch his mop. Maisie dashed after him but she tripped over his bucket and toppled into the pool. She was panic-stricken! She couldn't swim and, like all little kittens, she hated water. She pawed at the water furiously, mewing with fright, and all at once she realised she was keeping afloat and moving along.

SHE WAS SWIMMING!

When Mr Whiskers came back, he couldn't believe his eyes. There was Maisie, fully dressed, pussy-paddling along in the school pool!

He groaned.

"Not you again, Maisie. Were you feeling hot, or just fed up with doing sums this morning?"

"Can you help me out please?" cried Maisie. "I fell in."

Mr Whiskers reached out a paw and lifted her onto the pool-side.

She was a sorry sight, all bedraggled, and pools of water dripped from her fur—but she was smiling!

She handed him a soggy piece of paper.

"I'm sorry your note got a wee bit wet," she said. "It says 15 bottles of milk for Miss Purrvis."

And before Mr Whiskers could say a word, Maisie dashed off to her classroom.

She opened the door wide and stood there, beaming.

"I've got wonderful news, Miss Purrvis," she announced. "I've learned how to swim!"

Maisie spent the rest of the morning by the fire in Mr Whiskers office wrapped in a big towel while her clothes dried out on the radiator.

No one seemed impressed by her wonderful news!

She wasn't allowed out at Playtime. Instead, she had to explain everything to Miss Purrvis, and listen while Miss Purrvis explained to her how dangerous it can be for little kittens to fall into swimming pools.

Then Miss Purrvis fetched Maisie's play-piece along to the office.

Mr Whiskers gave her some tea out of his flask, and Mr Rafferty gave her a pandrop when he came in to collect his Lollipop.

When her clothes were dry, Maisie got dressed with Miss Purrvis's help.

"Try to look before you leap next time, Maisie," said her teacher, "and you'll learn to keep out of hot water!"

Maisie agreed. She'd been in enough hot water recently to last her for a long time.

Life at school grew more and more exciting.

CHRISTMAS WAS COMING!

Maisie's class painted lovely big pictures to decorate the hall.

Granny and Mrs McKitty bought tickets for the school concert. Maisie wouldn't tell them what she was doing in the concert but said they would get a surprise.

Miss Purrvis introduced the Show.

Everyone was excellent. Kittens danced, kittens sang, and some told jokes and recited poems.

There was no sign of Maisie yet.

Then a huge Chinese dragon danced on, jumping and twisting, with lots of paws peeping out from underneath. It came down from the stage and wound in and out amongst the audience, to the accompaniment of drums and gongs.

Granny tried hard to see if she could see Maisie's paws, but the dragon was too quick.

Everyone clapped and cheered as it danced off again.

Then, last of all, came a little choir of Angels, singing a Christmas carol.

Mrs McKitty was amazed.

There in the front row, singing so sweetly, was Maisie.
She sang a Carol all by herself.

This was Granny's proudest moment! Maisie was upsides
with Lydia MacSporran at last!

Lydia couldn't sing for toffee!

Next day was the class Christmas party—lots of games as well
as jelly, ice cream, crackers and cake.

Then the lights were turned down and Santa Claus appeared carrying a big sack. He took each kitten on his knee, and had a word with them, then gave them a present.

When it was Maisie's turn, he asked her what she wanted for Christmas.

"Will I bring you a bike? Or a nice book?"

Maisie shook her head.

"I know what I'd really like, but it might be too difficult fetching him and squeezing him down the chimney."

"Tell me then," said Santa, "and I'll do my very best."

"I'd like my Daddy to come home and see me swimming. I haven't seen him for such a long time."

Santa gave her a present out of the sack, and said he would see what could be done.

When Maisie got home from the party, Granny gave her a cuddle and said,

"Take your paws and cover your eyes; Count to three and you'll get a surprise!"

When she opened her eyes there stood DADDY!

There were great celebrations at Granny's that night. They had so much to tell one another. Daddy drank six cups of Granny's delicious tea. He said he'd really missed it—and her cooking, too.

He was very proud when he saw Maisie's gold stars and heard she'd been an Angel in the school concert, but he was proudest of all to learn that she could swim! He thought it was wonderful news.

And it was Christmas Eve.

They each hung up a stocking, and Daddy helped Maisie to lay out a plate of goodies for Santa. Then, after telling her a lovely story about a Yak who liked Haggis, he tucked her in and kissed her Good-night.

As she fell asleep, Maisie was the happiest kitten in the world.

Glossary:

brae	hill
pandrop	peppermint sweet
Petticoat Tails	shortbread
play-piece	snack
tatties	potatoes
tickled	pleased
wee	small